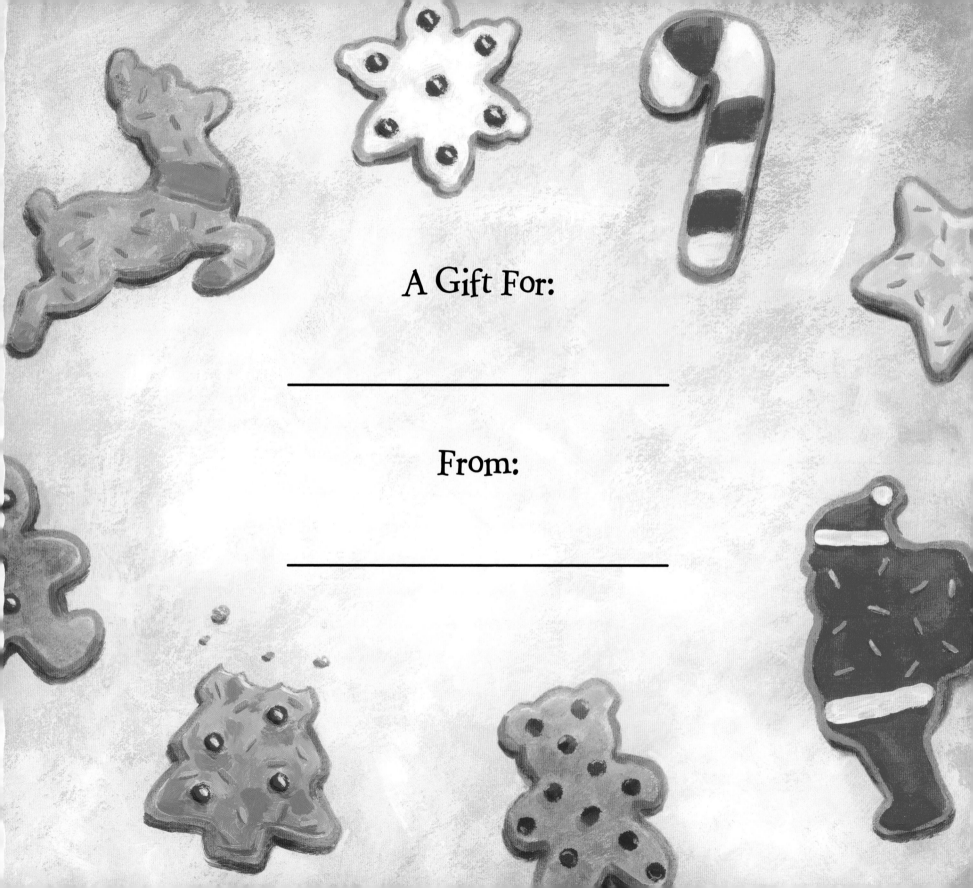

A Gift For:

_____

From:

_____

Copyright © 2015 Hallmark Licensing, LLC

Published by Hallmark Gift Books,
a division of Hallmark Cards, Inc.,
Kansas City, MO 64141
Visit us on the Web at Hallmark.com.

Editorial Director: Delia Berrigan
Editor: Kim Schworm Acosta
Art Director: Jan Mastin
Production Designer: Dan Horton

ISBN: 978-1-59530-765-1
XKT1124

Printed and bound in China
JUL15

There's Snow Time Like Cookie Time!

Written by Suzanne Heins and Andrew Blackburn
Illustrated by Mike Esberg

Cookies were Snowfred's most favorite food.

And Christmastime always put him in the mood

for a cookie . . . or seven, or maybe a dozen!

(If that's hard to believe, just ask Crystal, his cousin.)

One morning, Snowfred sniffed something so sweet
that it knocked his snow stockings right off his snow feet.
And he knew right away—it just had to be cookies!
After all, Snowfred wasn't a smell-sniffing rookie.

SNIFF
SNIFF

Sprinting past stockings and dodging the tree,

he and his little dog, Rex, ran to see

who in the kitchen was tempting them so.

His mother was there, rolling out cookie dough.

"I'm sorry, Snowfred," she said to her son.
"No eating cookies—not even just one!
They're all for the cookie fair later today
when Mittenville's best will be out on display!"

Leaving the kitchen, his tummy was rumbly.
Snowdrop, his sister, who saw he was grumbly,
suggested some skating might help him unwind.
But nothing could get cookies off Snowfred's mind.

"Snowfred," his father said, "come help me, please!
We need some more lights on our house and our trees!"

"How lovely!" Dad said. "See how everything twinkles?"
But Snowfred just saw sparkly cookies with sprinkles!

His brother named Shiverton said with a snort,
"Come on, now, Snowfred! Let's build us a fort!"
Afterward, Shiverton said, "Snowfred, lookee!
Why is your side shaped like one giant cookie?"

He sledded. He snowballed. He rode in a sleigh.
And Snowfred survived the whole cookie-less day.

He honestly hadn't believed he could do it.

But evening had come before he even knew it!

It was just about time for the town's cookie fair.

Soon the sweet smell of cookies would be in the air!

Snowfred walked in the door and sniffed such an aroma—
the best smell from Snow York down to old Snowklahoma!
But the kitchen was empty—no cookies were there!
Could they all just have vanished right into thin air?

Then, his mother stepped forward. "I have to admit—
I snuck one and then two. Then I just couldn't quit!"

"I ate some, too," said his dad to his mother.

"Me, three!" said his sister. "Me, four!" said his brother.

"Oh, Snowfred," his mom said. "I asked you to wait.

But the rest of us couldn't! We ate and we ate!

I'm sorry we couldn't stop once we began."

But Snowfred said, "That's OK. I've got a plan."

"I may be the world's number one cookie-eater.

But being with you guys is fifty times sweeter!

So let's make some more! And this time they'll be better.

Because this time we'll make every cookie together."

If this tasty adventure warmed your heart,
or if perhaps you just liked the art,
we would love to hear from you.

PLEASE SEND YOUR COMMENTS TO:
Hallmark Book Feedback
P.O. Box 419034
Mail Drop 100
Kansas City, MO 64141

OR E-MAIL US AT:
booknotes@hallmark.com